By Nicholas Jordon Blackburn

WARNING THIS BOOK IS PROPAGANDA

Even the smallest act of service, the simplest act of kindness, is a way to honor those we lost, a way to reclaim the spirit of unity that followed 9/11.

—Barack Obama

Copyright 2019 by Nicholas Jordon Blackburn

Cover and interior designed by Nicholas Jordon Blackburn
Cover Art contributed by Toria Jordan Nagel
Edited by Rachael Jordan Blackburn

All rights reserved. No part of this book may be reproduced or transmitted in any form or by any means, electronic or mechanical, including photocopying, recording or by any information storage and retrieval system, without written consent from the publisher, except for the brief quotes in review.

This book was published by Zinci Media

I DEDICATE THIS BOOK TO MY FIRST INFLUENCER, MY MOTHER, WHO ALWAYS TOLD ME TO MARCH TO THE BEAT OF MY OWN DRUMMER. I LOVE YOU BUNCHES, AND BUNCHES, AND MORE THAN THAT.

#BUYMYBOOK

Poets challenge socials norms
Through hope and scorn
While our brains are raging
Like a coastal storm
We can see beauty in
The rose's thorns
Or rows of corn
We're known to mourn
In reverie like a blowing horn
Emotions known to swell up
Faster than a locust swarm

We are the walkers of hot coals
We speak through the wire
Our road's paved with pot holes
Lanes filled with stupid drivers

Our challenge in life
Is to take on
Every challenge in life
And still balance the light
With the dark my talent ignites
My spark gives me strength
When I'm down in a fight
Gives me the feeling that
I can grow talons and flight
Might actually be possible
In truth it's my fountain of life
You can keep your youth
I feel astoundingly light

To view the summit
Of the mountain despite
Taking the road less traveled

We need a Walt Whitman
Another Edgar Allen Poe
Those willing to drown in woes
Then put it down in prose
Find insights in the highest heights
And profoundest lows
To describe the beauty of beaches
Where they've found their toes

To quote like half of hip hop
We are the last of a dying breed
Feel out of place like we stepped
Straight out of a time machine
Never admire a miser
We try to squeeze
Every last tiny piece
Of life before we expire
Only hope is to die in peace
So we live defiantly
With a belly full of fire
Like our intestines were a pyre

We can be both kind and mean
Poets are the kind who dream
Of finding gleam in another's eyes
Like they're a child swinging wildly
From an oak tree with a tire swing
Dreaming they can fly

#YOLO

O' Captain, my Captain
Atop my desk I stand
O' Captain my Captain
Heart with chest in hand
O' Captain my Captain
Let us seize the day
O' Captain my Captain
I'll let you lead the way
O' Captain my Captain

I am a dead poet
Skin shed throw it
Instead Thoreau it
Like Henry David
Give hope to hopeless
Send me sacred quotes
You wrote with
Endless envy naked
Soaking in a bathtub
Dreaming of back rubs
O' Captain my Captain

Let me hear
Your barbaric yawps
Scream till the wheels
On the Ferris stop
Need a day like Ferris off
Back when my cheeks
We're bare and soft

In class staring off
Into the abyss
Trying to resist
Caring wearing off
O' Captain my Captain

It seems every few years
I'll put down the pen
Only to find shadows
Surrounding then
Head pounding in
I slip below the surface
Ready to drown again
Then I surface with purpose
Never down for ten counts
O' Captain my Captain

I use these words
To woo women
Into the nude sinning
Sipping brew with 'em
I'm too confused to vent an
Ounce of this brewed venom
Then feud with 'em again
Acting rude then I'm out
O' Captain my Captain

Forgive this starving artist
I've reaped the Harbingers Harvest
I opened Pandora's Box
I once fed a vampire garlic

Frankly I don't give a damn Scarlett
If you think I lived like a harlot
I'll sing my song like a hymn
Until I'm gone with the wind
O' Captain my Captain

Poets aren't cool anymore
We used to be the bees knees
Replaced by James Hardin and CP
Steph Curry shooting deep threes
Got us begging like please read
You don't know the wounds
I opened in order
For you to read these

O' Captain, my Captain
Atop my desk I stand
O' Captain my Captain
Heart with chest in hand
O' Captain my Captain
Let us seize the day
O' Captain my Captain
I'll let you lead the way
O' Captain my Captain

#SAVAGE

I make no apologies
For being less than scholarly
When I weigh in on policy
Its safe to assume probably
Sometimes I lack in modesty
I'm a bleeding heart
Like they're slashing arteries
A part of me is starved for peace
A part of me is a starving beast
Willing to feast on entrails partially
Inhaling darkness has hardened me
I'm a walking contradiction
With a mission to use my diction
To add friction to the superficial
Like I launched a nuclear missile
At you racist whistling Dixie
I'm the flip side of the coin
A skateboarding devils advocate
Ready to flip the deck
On these fascist pigs
Don't mistake my passion if
You get on my bad side
My attitude's a snapping whip
If you start flapping lips
Call me a savage if
I preach what I'm practicing
While I seek to be a pacifist
I'm not meek you see my passion lifts
My spirit up if I ever lack for it
I learned to find solace

In the law of averages
To grab me from the blackest pit
Not just talking shit I back it with
Tactics aimed at poking ribs
Like I'm Wayne Brady
Bought to choke a bitch
While I'm seek redemption
Like my alias was Tacitus
Then I match it with a tacit wit
When I'm blasting hits on I-9
Like we're playing battleships
Let that last one sink in…

Looking at the limelight like
I want to bask in that
Flow like water was
My natural habitat
I keep it action packed
Sitting in a masterclass
Looking for the banners
That these rafters lack
I've been on this jagged path
Since the cabbage patch
As a kid in Rabbit Hash
Studying to practice math
Smile quick and laughing fast
Eating a bag of Cracker Jacks
Trying to do numbers like Captain Jack
Or Gandalf with a magic staff
Bet one day I'll have a lavish pad
When I flip words like half a pack
Strapped to the back of acrobats

I'm so ready to blow like c4
Wired to a blasting cap
You don't want none
I come to the battle strapped
With a battle axe imagine that
You opened Pandora's box
With no way to latch it back
I'm sorry but I have to ask
Didn't you consider the aftermath?
You got my attention
Hoping to pass it fast
Like we're playing hot potato
And you want to pass it back
I treat it like a smash and grab
Throw a straight at your face
Followed with a savage jab
Spit like Ken Kaniff
While I rip a riff
Like I'm Back in Black
Leave you needing a Maxi pad
I'm low key acting like Loki
Really I'm just after laughs
Add a chick with the fattest ass
Pardon me for acting crass
I could use a Baptist bath
Or an acid tab to snap me back
We all need a moment to act an ass
My other persona took over my body
But now he's saying I can have it back

#VIRAL

I know I've got no hope of going viral
I don't rope-a-dope or throw a spiral
I won't stoke a hoax or host denials
I hope to go from coast to coast
From the big city to the broken silos
Giving out hope and smiles
To those who know the road
Filled with lows and woes
You've chose to roam
Riding on broken spokes
You know the cycle
Is endless so I'm penning a sentence
Knowing I'll be sentenced in a open trial
Hope they look back and say I spoke with guile
I know some will say I'm so entitled
I befriended demons like the omen child
That I'm a poser while I'm really
Humpty Dumpty with a broken smile
Jesus how many rhymes do I need to fit
Before these ceaseless twits
Plead the fifth or ease their grip
My easel sits in evil pits
As well as where eagle's sit
Equipped with lethal wit
Sick as measles gets
More than probably
My drive is like I chug
Diesel with my morning coffee
Looking for a box office hit
Then come equipped

With the sequel's script
Then throw in a prequel pitch
Get it... throw a pitch
Doesn't count if you don't notice it
I wrote this with the hope it gets
The attention it deserves
The chosen kid unloading quips
The Iliad with a Homer Simps
And the Frozen chick
As a throw in twist
Got them all throwing fits
Like I wrote this shit
For M. Night Shyamalan
I'm hoping this catches fire
Like a batch of tires
Soaking in gasoline
Notice I've been practicing
Let the wind catcher catch my dream
I promise I won't act obscene
I'll probably laugh and scream
Like a batch of batshit
Crazy ratchet queens
With a magic gleam in my eyes
Like i can't believe it's happening
It's to fast I mean
The views are climbing
Faster than a track meet
I started writing when I had acne
I put in 10 thousand hours
Now I'm feeling sassy
If you @ me laughing
This black sheep is actually

Actively offering only pitfalls
I should probably be penned off
It's like I can't turn my pen off
You may be swayed to say
I sure play a mean pin ball
So dope you could hear a pin fall
What you pen is awful
That sin'll cost you
Like the Pentecostals
This sinner's gospel
Mocks you with gusto
Strike from the shadows
Dropped with a cut throat
Got Scooby yelling Rut Roh
Got Shaggy running tuck tail
Got me like Scrooge McDuck
In the intro from Duck Tails
Spit this shit like make a wish
You're my genie in a bottle
So if you get a whiff of this
And you give a shit
Hit or click to like and follow
Leave a comment
Help me gain some traction
Not searching for fame
Just trying to flame my passion
Set off a chain reaction
Create change in actions
Like a rogue disciple
Picture the moment I go
From no one to a glowing idol
If only I had any hope of going viral

#DRACARYS

I was born partially deaf
Life dealt the hand
This was part of the deck
School was a challenge
It was my hardest yet
I needed speech classes
To pronounce R's and S
Getting trounced in a race
That I hadn't started yet
Like the Tortoise and Hare
With my shoes strings tied
Damn rabbit without a care
Watch him go whooshing by
I lacked the foundation
That language was built
As I progressed in school
I saw how the angle would tilt
Trying to find a foothold
But it was like dancing in stilts
Still I was determined
I said I can and I will
Find a way to manage this hill
Without the Jack and Jill
Use a cannon to build
A staircase from stone
Or plant a seed like I'm
Planning to till a beanstalk
Turn the world make believe
My momma always had faith in me
That's how I know fate's decreed

I cut my own path
From the day I was born
To the day I wear a toe tag
I know inside of me
Is a Magnum Opus
I know if my motives
Match my passion
The potential
Has the potency
To be explosive
Like Ye and Jay
When they wrote "Otis"
Hold on
Better throw ya robe on
I'm not going to
Watch the throne
I'm going Drogon
Till its dripping iron
'Cause death can get you
Quick as Qyburn
So I'm passing in oncoming
Traffic like I hit the siren
I'm coming through
You coming too?
I got my crew
You can get behind them
Not trying to be
Another starving artist
Or the type to write
But won't let people see
A piece of guarded parchment
So I treat these obstacles

Like a barrier with a barbed fence
Plant a charge
Make a breech
Ready my breath
Then charge in
Wearing these scars
Carved into skin in stark tints
With a pride only felt by those
Who've traversed the darkness

Dracarys

I found the greatest gift
I can give is let my light shine
I was scared for thirty years
Walking a tight rope of light twine
Before I found a life line
It helped pull me out of the pit
I went in a fool
Came out with some grit
Belt with more tools
And a talent for wit
I just had to embrace
My talent again
When I needed strength
I dug deep in my ugly
And found it within
When I conquered my demons
I was just as astounded as them

#THROWBACKTHURSDAY

When I was a child my mouth
Was on cruise control doing 120
I was a big spender splurging
Every cent of my lunch money
I was a thumb sucker
It was my first pacification
I never lacked for tact
For lack of imagination

I'd escaped in an endless
Wonderland of fantasy
Like ants with dancing feet
While the DJ's sampling
Ample amounts of insanity
Manically under a canopy
Of leaves can't you see it?

I was a free spirit
My arms wings
Flapping frantically
Climbing every tree
Like no fall could damage me
I loved the way the forest
Always offered amnesty
The call of the wild
Was always there to answer me

Now I'm older
I shoulder responsibility willingly
I can tell you when my will
To be a silken king
Wilted like a willow tree
When the stream began filtering
Oil and water from a busted pipeline
They said wouldn't break

I was taught to speak the truth from adults ironically
Lying is a disease that adults suffer chronically
If it wasn't all so tragic I'd suspect this a comedy
Holding my breath for "Who throws a shoe? Honestly!"

I think the world needs the international man of mystery
To come out of retirement and free us of our misery
We could use a bit more wizardry and less bigotry
Can we quit allowing for the rise of the lizard king?

I wanna go back when
Captain Planet was teaching love
When Timone and Pumba
Showed a king eating slugs
Was a means for grub
Singing Hakuna Matada
What a wonderful way to live

#ITSCOMPLICATED

We act like we're fine
But we both know it's a lie
Notice when your in sight
I can't focus my mind
One way like a locomotive
Smoke rolling behind
The joke is this ridiculous
Hocus pocus disguise
I don't know if it's wise
To rope a dope this prose
Or let it soak up in lye
Let Zeus open the sky
Lightning rolling on by
Tears soaking my eyes

They get wiped away
Twice a day suffice to say
This might be wrong
But it feels right today
In darkness begging
You to light the way
I don't know if it's right
To reignite the flames
Heart ready to fight my brain
You'd think I like the pain
The definition of insanity
I'd like to change

You think I'm Icarus
Flying high with wax wings

Plummeting back to earth
Around the time I was last seen
Getting so sick of this
Role as the black sheep
Falling without a net
Hoping that you'll catch me
I already caught you
Red handed

DON'T LIE TO ME!!!!!

I went through your phone
I saw you text your ex
Tell me the truth
What am I second best
I already saw the thread
Before you crawled into bed
So don't say it's all in my head
You said you'd help me out with school
When I went back to serving

WHAT THE FUCK!!!!!!

You intentionally took
This path to hurt me
It all makes sense now
I get why you've been acting surly
You cut me open and bled me dry
I'm falling victim to your taxidermy

I'M SORRY!!!!!!

I didn't mean to scream
I know this seems obscene
But if you didn't act
Like a preening teen
I wouldn't have to yell
And demean your dreams
Until you're a shell
Of a human being
Sometimes it seems
We're the basis for an episode
Of King of Queens

BABY I LOVE YOU!!!!!!!!

I just want to go back to that first week
Go back to our first date
The reason you chose me in the first place
When your kisses felt like earthquakes
Before I had to save face
Before you had second thoughts
Before another lesson taught
In humility writing soliloquy's
Back when you chilled with me
So willingly spilling beans
We we're really free
Now you forgot how
To be real with me and I hate it
I hate it 'cause now I have to face this
Inevitability mimicking stability
Smiling like I donned a face lift
And when my friends ask
I just say it's complicated

#SWIPERIGHT

I was up late night bored
So I started swiping
Flipping through chicks
Like a water bison
Left, left, left, right, left
Yes, yes, yes I guess
Then I got an alert I found a match
Sent a message like hey girl
What makes you frown and laugh
Asked if she wanted to get a drink
Throw it down the hatch
I don't have a mound of cash
But there is a bar down the way
The bouncer lets me slip around the back
So we can skip the cover charge
We planned to meet in a couple of days
Hoping cupid strings his supple bow
And sends a couple of strays
My way I could use some luck
Told my dude I met this chick
On Tinder she's cute as fuck
Check out this pic of her
Thats her throwing duces up
This chick got my fuses lit
No use in defusing it
She's blowing up my phone
I think I could get used to this
I haven't text back that much
I'm trying to play it cool
She could be Princess Zelda

With endless links to her chain of fools
I'm waiting for a bit to get some leverage
Biding time to craft the perfect message
For her to digest it like...
Try as I might I can't help it
I'm addicted to your smiling face
I'd run miles for a bouquet of flowers
Hoping to brighten your day
Tell me what will lighten your load?
What's the price to be paid?
No dammit that's too cliche
Sounds like I'll keep a lock of hair
In a locket for a keepsake
What if I said...
Call me old fashioned
Call me a hopeless romantic
Call this the law of attraction
Call it a seed I'm hoping gets planted
Call me when the moon is out
Call when the sun kisses the horizon
Call when you're ready to switch
Like the dude with Verizon
If you're sick of your ex's shit
He's got your head spinning
Like this is the Exorcist
Asking yourself if this
Is the best it gets
Wondering if this is a test
Then this should be considered
My testament of form
Against your former
No that won't work it's too wordy

I'll come off too nerdy
But I could say something like
I'm not your average joe
Looking for photos with a lavish pose
Only wanting to smash and go
Like he's playing wack a mole
So tell me what it takes
How about a magic prose
To capture your sense of rapture
With a practiced flow
No… no! That won't… Damn it
I don't understand it
How do people manage
To press their advantage
Television made me think it was easy
To find both love and quicksand
Then the internet gave us Tinder
Swiping right with quick hands
I'm just trying to sound like I have quick wit
She's probably just hoping its not a dick pic
She won't be prepared for my over share
I'll probably scare her off before the date
She'll think I'm the next Norman Bates
Or Ramsey Bolton come to storm the gates
What if I said call me George you can be my Judy Jetson
No OMG that's so dumb that's out of the question
Let me delete all of this before I press send

#LOVEATFIRSTSIGHT

We got to the bar at like 10:30
I didn't have a ton of cash
I had to pay my rent early
We went to this one place
Where I knew the barkeep
I planned to pay for drinks
And hoped she wasn't starving
We walked in she to went straight to the dance floor
Looking at me like you about to dance or…
Should I get another you know it takes two to tango
I said I hear the sax and drums but my rhythm's anglo
So if you had high expectations I suggest you aim low
She pulled me close and danced unchained like Django
Then went to the bar and ordered a White Claw Mango
In the background there was bad karaoke
Blaring while I was low key staring
Thinking O' please don't make me sing
I needed a distraction so I ordered a Berliner Vice
I was still at the bar when it was her turn on the mic
It was like someone turned on a light
She shined like a torch burns in the night
She sang me a song and I started fallen
Like I was on a date with Alicia Keys
I'm not religious but I was like Jesus please
I'll believe in thee if this angel leaves with me
She got off the stage came over and said I need to pee
I was enthralled watching her walk away in sequin jeans

When she came back I said
Maybe Maybelline made me believe
In unattainable beauty
But If I may be so bold
You've got beauty usually
Reserved for what an easel holds
Got me thinking how steeples tolls
White doves white dress as people hold
The train up like a robbery
And people throw rice as we drive away
With cans clacking on the blacktop
With mountains in the backdrop
The look in her face told me to back off
Then she laughed and called me a jack off
She said the bartenders bitching
Been a while since last call

Here was my moment of truth
Years spent honed in my youth
My chest was pounding like a drum
I couldn't keep my heart stable
She grabbed my hand
I folded like a card table
She grinned as I pulled her in
While I gripped her hips I dipped her
And kissed her like Clark Gable

We walked through the streets
We talked through the night
We didn't stop till the light
Rose in the east
And birds hopped into flight

I'd make an obscure reference
You were still quick with the banter
Come through slick with an answer
Quick like a dancer or an Olympic
Sticking the landing you're so graceful
Unless you've been drinking
Then you look like a baby giraffe
Trying to find it's legs

Your sense of humor is tasteless
Purple polka dot socks were your favorite
Your soul seems so endlessly passionate
Like to play fight for fun or a match of wits
You like to use my words against me
Like we were playing a game of scrabble
Asked where have all the cowboys gone
Then we jumped in the saddle
We rode as the sun rose, until it set in the west
Painting pastel views the way only the dessert attests
Confess I wasn't looking for the pleasures of flesh
They say the crazier she is the better the sex
The first time I told you I loved you I said it in jest
Nevertheless that moment when
Your head was pressed to my chest
My arm was falling asleep
But I kept letting you rest
Watching the rise and fall
Of the breath in your chest
I knew at the moment
With the only exception of death
That I would love you forever

#FOREVER

It all started with a toothbrush
That first sign I was yours
And you were mine
Then socks got left
Two at a time
Crumbled in a pile
On my bedroom floor
The view was divine
Purple polka dots
Set against faded black
Next to your favorite slacks
I've returned them twice
But they've made it back
How great is that?

Soon that toothbrush
That turned into socks
That turned into a dresser
That turned into dinner with your folks
That felt like a super bowl presser
Even your Dad was impressed
At how I handled the pressure
Then you grabbed me by the neck
And kissed me sweeter than nectar

I watched our wedding videos
Again just last week
I'll never forget that moment
When the pastor asked me
If I'll take care of you

Both in sickness and in health
I didn't know then the implications
The situation called for a toast
And we all cheered like cheers
Was still in syndication
You flipped flying flowers
To friends over your head
We didn't go to the mountains
We went to the ocean instead
The honey moon spent
Mostly close to the bed

Thirty years later we had a family
Our home was bought and paid for
It was just another routine checkups
That told us you were stage four
The Doctor said it was too late
He wished he could say more
I brought your toothbrush to the hospital
So you could have something to feel like home
I told her this was just another obstacles
And I 'd be damned if I'd let her face it alone

I stayed in your room
I slept on that couch
I watched you slip away
I couldn't stay in our house
I had to be there
I had to hold your hand
Who else was going to
Play your favorite bands
You always seemed more at ease

With Florence and the Machines
You loved the way Alicia poured her soul
Whenever she played the keys
You'd sing along stayed in key
Rocking purple polka dot socks
I'd watch as you swayed your feet
While in my head I hear
Sam Smith begging please
Won't you stay with me

But prayers didn't save you
I still stay and read
The letter you left
Telling me how that first night
With your head on my chest
How you said under breath
That you loved me and if I'd heard it
You'd just say you said it in jest
That nevertheless at that moment
You knew you'd love me forever

I still keep your toothbrush
Over on the bathroom sink
Reminds how your smile
Would make a black room gleam
I keep it as a reminder
So during my mourning routine
I find my smile again
If only in for a blink

#SEMICOLON

It took a long time for me to say I was suicidal
Emotions came through in tidal waves
To say I'm too entitled
While I'm looking up to a noose
Like I was some crude disciple
I think I need newer idols
I'm not up to the task at hand
Watching social apps these people jacked and tan
Hit the slopes in Aspen, then red eye to bask in sand
With a glass of jack in hand relax and fan themselves
While I'm in hell comparing my timeline to theirs
Trying to share for likes but lies are ensnared
Go to foot locker snap a pic when I try on a pair
They told me fake it till you make it so I smile a lot
No one sees the trials I've fought like a daredevil
The miles I've lost In a haze with my thoughts black
The cost for denial is not to be scoffed at
I set out searching for Herculean fame
But wound up just circling the drain
Trust me I get all the frustration
I know I over react without qualification
You might want to call in a shaman
I know I'm not east to deal with
That's why I'm calling for patience

After graduation thought it be like heaven
Not facing over saturation in the job market
Plus impatient bastards waiting
To snatch up my lack of savings
For student loans before my feet

Have even smacked the pavement
They're ready to ask for payment
Then task a fascist layman
To dismantle protections
And you have the unmitigated gall
To ask why I'm back on payments
And question my lack of patience

Mother fucker I'm ready to shank it out
If I get one more over-drafted bank account
I'm working over forty hours a week
Side hustles and a nine to five
You might see me on diners and dives
Serving a pint and fries as I try to scry
Why this guy is being such a prick
I know he isn't about to leave a tip
I need this job but I don't need this shit
I need to keep my mouth shut
Like I'm about to plead the fifth

If I'm being honest
I'm depressed as fuck
Nothing really interest me
About to be Sum 41 year old in too deep
Constantly being chased by endless sleep
I'm socially awkward but social media
Got me in 2D looking like the Sims
Smiling like sins too cheap to bother
I hope you follow my bread crumbs
Everyone says the light's shining
But all I can see is red rum
Crippling chaos, commotion, and bedlam

If god created this it must be a test run
I quietly get anxiety
Every time I try and speak
Self medicating, fuck sobriety, fuck society
If god made me he must of fucked the wiring

I didn't plan to be a pessimist
But there's only so many times
That you can step in shit
Until your left with this
Existential question
About if life is just a quest to get
A XO stencil and a pencil to leverage it
Is this the best it gets?
Live, love, work then death
Comes collecting its due
I don't even know who
I'm posing this question to
No ones up there listening
Glistening in white robes
While we're down here traversing
Like acrobats on a tight rope

I'm sending out an SOS like message in a bottle
Life is a bottled lined beach both blessed and awful
Bite the bullet but better be ready for the kickback
Beautiful bliss blesses us all the with the same gift bag

Moments before a leap of faith I can feel my palms sweating
Tell the priest I've made my peace time to get the psalms ready

#MYRELIGIONISLOVE

Im not religious
But if I was
My religion
Wouldn't worship
Or morph its lore
To send warships
Towards distant lands
Who couldn't afford
Your lordships bathrobe

My religion
Wouldn't force its delegates
To relish in embellishments
Selling their celibate
But seldom is
Lets be real

My religion
Isn't hypocritical
Even if sometimes I am
My religion evolves with me
Across my life span
Its my peaceful place
Mine involves white sand
With my soulmate on my left arm
And spiced rum in my right hand

My religion
Teaches empowerment
And plenty of humility

Come chill with me
Let a soliloquy fill my speech
With the thrills they seek
Really we all are just seeking truth

My religion uses rhymes as its vessel
My religion doesn't have a God or a Devil
No holy men with rocks in their bezel
From profits embezzled
Got locks on the temple
And blocks on your mental
Free your mind

My religion doesn't create separation
We're all singing the same songs
Just listening to separate stations
To many people are obsessed
Stressed and less than patient
When at the end of the day
We all confess the same sins

My religion likes how we are alike
Yet loves how we're different
My religion is never bugged
At a shrug of indifference

My religion doesn't condemn love
Even if between the same sex
No hate or looking who to blame next
We all think we have the answers
We just don't all have the same test

Its all contextual
Taking text out of context
To pull blessed wool
Over people's eyes
By those claiming
They possess the truth
But really need to check their ego
The Vatican has more priceless art
Then they know what to do with
But they're still collecting G notes
All the while my neighbor
Is injecting needles
I'm checking peepholes
For people possessed with evil
Willing to shoot you down
Then direct the sequel

My religion
Doesn't protect from evil
My religion doesn't blame
My religion doesn't shoot
My religion doesn't claim
To be the only truth

Religion has become our great divide
Religion has become a reason for violence
Religion has become a tool of tyrants
Religion has torn families apart
Religion has also made them whole

Honestly I have no idea
If religion can save your soul

Raise the dead or even pave a hole
What I do know is religion
Is only what you make it
I do know that people who take it
And reshape it for personal gain
Should be ashamed to deface it
For baseless aspirations
Creating another disaster
Waiting to happen
All to hasten happenstance
For passion at a glance
Packed with saturation
That will never be my religion
My religion teaches peace
Above all my religion teaches love
My religion teaches
We can all be gods
Without the push and shove
My religion is my religion
Though its no religion at all
Religion is a barrier
And my religion
Prays all the barriers fall

#JESUSSAVES

They say…

The meek shall inherit the earth
The weak got demerits at birth
The sleek will embarrass your worth
They preach to prepare us in church

What's worse than a preacher ensnared in his purse
The root of all evil like he ain't aware of the curse
Mama said hope for the best and prepare for the worst
Get a golden casket like we're prepared for the dirt

Acting pious while asking Midas to the secret of life
Congregation praying for relief to the strife
Mega church conmen acting like a thieves in the night
While the parishioners struggle to keep on the lights

These excuses are starting to feel quite contrived
Like a likelihood of a better livelihood tied to tithes
So my hard earned paying for jets to ride the skies
Instead of paying for families everyday grinding by

And you wonder why I wont step foot in your holy place
Like you're holding the only keys to the pearly gates
When I'm just feeding your needs for earthly tastes
Bestowing upon you blessings that you will surely waste

I'd be better off in the soup kitchen filling ladles
Than stories of God convincing Kane of killing Able
It was cute when it was still all a children's fable

Before you bought a new Coup De Ville in sable
To go with the two thoroughbreds in the stable

You might convince me if you weren't ignoring the
Basics tenants of that which you're imploring me
It makes you look like an backward ass acting ornery
Keep your damnation I don't acknowledge your authority

Lord forgive me I get enraged at hypocrisy
Watch them play the telephone game with a prophecy
The sole holders of truth like they own a monopoly
When statistics say they will soon be obsolete

I'm not against the church I'm against their perversions
Does the preacher feel guilt when scripting a sermon
Just a prick of concern when so fixed and determined
Thinking of choir boys licking lips like a serpent

They say he without sin shall cast the first stone
No one speaks up since we all live in glass homes
Hear the sounds of silence without Simon and G
Feeling disturbed like lions are leading the sheep

#SEPARATIONOFEARTHANDHATE

I want to be an optimist
But I don't know if
Its possible to stop this ship
We won't acknowledge
When non-profits
Are tax exempt
But have lobbyist
In every lobby, hearing
And backroom in politics
Spitting derision while
We're the ones who swallow it

Y'all getting pissed ready to see us off
So you can enact Christian Sharia Law
It's kinda sad you don't see the parallels
Or if you do you aren't prepared to tell

Are our views so entrenched?
Are we so crude in defense
That we simply choose malcontent
Instead of diffuse now and then?

The situation is getting critical
Y'all wanna get biblical
But this country was founded
By people fleeing religious oppression
So your obsession about my indiscretions
Don't come into question
When The House is in session

I won't tell you what you can preach
But you can't tell public school
Teachers what they can teach
You can't tell doctors how they can heal
When we signed our independence
That shit wasn't apart of the deal

Separation of church and state
Was the mortar to our foundation
Now the grounds breaking
As deep rooted hate threatens
To add cracks and breaks
Quick someone grab the masking tape
We need a bat with a mask and cape
Throw in a cat Anne Hathaway
Or The volleyball from Castaway
Because everyone needs a friend

For those of us lacking faith
We've had debates using facts to sate
Your rhetoric but your tactics lately
Are competitive the ways it's repetitive
Hoping to win through use of sedatives
You can't lull me to sleep instead of it
I'm getting in the driver's seat and revving it
I'm ready to grab a medic's kit
And shock the system

Stop and listen
I'm not mocking Christians
I'm saying your holy book
Has no place in debate

You've given hatred a face
Trying to put the Gays in their place
You didn't wanna bake 'em a cake
So they could celebrate but couldn't
Because of your lack of understanding
An obvious lack of empathy
Worst of all for lack of love
You have my honest sympathy

Change isn't always
Easy to deal with
I don't judge you
I want to help you
You want to hate me
I want to love you

I'm an active pacifist
And this is about as
Passive as it gets
I have a massive savage stick
But I'm offering the carrot
With blasphemous tact and wit
Mostly because I know
No matter what I do
To frame or bracket this
You'll still be acting pissed
All to believe in a Pastor with
Overly passionate magic tricks

#METOO

Tears streaming makeup compromised
Hair in disarray left with two swollen eyes
Skirt hefted and her panties were ripped
Earlier that night she looked perfect
Getting ready for a night out with her friends
Until she found the devil in a serpent
As he touched her skin she felt a chill
She froze in the moment, well until
He started groping more aggressive
She was being undressed
She started to pull away
Fighting the stress
Rising cries of distress
He put a hand over her mouth
Then he started biting her neck
She shoved him as hard as she could
She hit him right in the chest
Her fight was inept as he pressed
His chest right to her flesh

If she's being honest
She was frozen but felt it
She was near unconscious
Afterwards emotions melted

She didn't know what to do
She didn't know who to tell
She went through it alone
Her own personal hell
She started cutting her self

She became the one in four
Felt the rise of fear whenever
A stranger was coming towards
Her in the street alone
While she's rummaged for
Mace or keys to poke
Him in the face
No need to know
If he's decent folk
If he doesn't give her space
He'll be bleeding slow

With her next lover
She constantly relives it
Every time she'd be under covers
She feels like she was undercover
In her own skin playing someone else
Someone who can enjoy being touched
Without wanting to jump

I've looked in their eyes
And felt defenseless
I didn't know what words to use
I don't know the verbiage to
Do just service to the pit in hell
I'd send those perverts to
I've seen the scars
I know who's hurting you
Pain is important
It deserves it due
But a time comes when
The bird has flew

Or it'll come back again
And fly over the nest cuckoo
Let me sit next to you
Offer a shoulder a vestibule
To a portal to the best of you

I know it's hard to trust guys
I don't know if I can help
But I'll sure a fuck try
Healing is a process
It's take a support system
The first person to find
Is someone who'll listen

To you non-believers
I'll put a halt to your boots
A man's more likely to get rapped
Than falsely accused

This goes out to
Dr Christine Blasey Ford
This is for Anita Hill
For every person pushing boulders
When they look and all they see is hills

This is for my mother
For both of my sisters
For every victims of #MeToo
If you need a sympathetic ear
I'm here and I believe you

#BLACKLIVESMATTER

You think we're alike because we match complexions
I think we've lost our way we should ask directions
Lessons in the past and present lack discretion
I hate to ask the question but how can you think you're better?

Ready to ratchet it up
More than half a tick
When you see a kneeling
Big afro'd Kaepernick
You get so mad you spit
Like it's blasphemous
He's a sack of shit
Kneeling during the anthem
Is sacrilege but ask if it's
About more than a pass and kick
If you'd move past the shit

He had y'all talking
For years even after
Spite the forest for paper
Then won't read a chapter

How many videos will go viral
Before we see its systemic
How many more Emmet's
Until we actually get it
Throw in a Timothy Thomas
Philando Castile, Tamir Rice
Don't forget about Trayvon

Can someone swap a suit
And throw a cape on

Can you keep up?
You sure your hands can hold it?
Now don't forget all the ones
That didn't have cameras rolling
Despite the damage I stand emboldened
Just look at the evidence
We set new precedence
When we as a people
Elected Barack as President

It's not race that separates
It's this caste system
Go back to past wisdom
Like Malcolm X or Dr King
Freshen up on the basics
See what they're offering

Think about how you'd react
When's Mars attack's
Aliens whip and scar your back
So you can harvest that
Garden patch starved and lacking
Basic decency but one day
A rebellion starts to sack
The plantation but your savior's skin
Is the darkest black

We're not that different just look past the foreground
Quit hanging onto traditions that need to be torn down

#GUNCONTROL

I'm stumped I need a "Country Road"
Take me home to a place
With gun control not a hundred souls
Pumped with holes on a summer stroll
But you're looking at me like a mummers farce
We are greater than this sum of parts
You're trying to pop my balloon
Like you're throwing a hundred darts
I wish someone would summons sparks
To light the dark before we come apart
We've had more mass shootings
Than days on the calendar
It's gotten to where it's feels
Like there is no place safe
Some act like it's no great weight
Willing you to see my side
Like a probate case
But you're not ready to read the message
Written in blood on walls and siding
On pavement where bodies fall inviting
A child a place to crawl she's hiding
Her face from all the fighting
You plead your case If we take
Guns from the law abiding
You'll leave them in the hands
Of all the wildlings
It's the precursor to a falling society
I think you need to pump the brakes
If we didn't make laws some would break
We'd have anarchy that's a dumb mistake

Like a movie shooting a hundredth take
Of the same scene on a green screen
But we're wresting death no special effects
Use this breath to attest our mettle suggest
We need new ways to cope
I'm searching for a ray of hope
Someone quick page the pope
We're choked with rage
So maybe if I say a joke
It might pave the road
Away from hate
Like Steve McQueen
In The Great Escape
We're jumping fences
A jarring landing might help
Some of y'all come to senses
We've become dumb defensive
I've become numb to thoughts and prayers
We need to get the cops and mayors
Stock brokers restaurant workers
And your awful neighbor
If you cut locks or toss a paper
Doesn't matter we need everyone
Carrying big sticks like hockey players
Maybe we should just go Bunraku
Get Josh Hartnett in a stunning coupe
Leading three hundred Spartans
The A team and The Expendables
Coming through to run a coup
Pulling up rolling down the window
Looking at you like you coming too?
Whatever it takes to come together

Show restraint or summon tethers
Treat mental health with a budget
Like we're funding war
Call these people terrorist
Like you've done before
If they were brown
No other way to face it down
How many more straying rounds
Laying down neighbors
Until we no longer bear arms
For the excuse of convention
We need new amendments
We need a new conviction
When Jesus faced crucifixion
He didn't get his crew to listen
To him spew derision
Like the Old Testament
He came with a new edition
Using truth imbued with wisdom
Talking to those who'd choose to listen
We got to stop acting like this
Is a problem that can't be solved
With a little more resolve
Get the masses standing stall
With uncanny gall demanding
Our government protect us
From threats of the interior
How many more mass shootings
How many more unlocked gun safes
How many more dead children
How many more until "some day"

#APPLEPIE

I was supposed to pay Kentucky
but somehow Ohio took it instead

I was gonna pay the phone bill
But that went to a roof over my head

I swear the gas bill is coming
I just put it in the mail

Whether it actually goes through
Now that's truly heads or tails

My auto insurance is on auto pay
It's sucking my bank account dry

All I do is work and go to school
My food is all greasy and fried

I was sold a dream about pastries
I fell for it but I don't know why

Nothing screams America!
Like fighting for a bigger slice of the pie

#FIGHTFOR15

I've heard your words
And I find your sermon lacks
Willing to spend a years pay
On a couple Birkin Bags
Then turn and laugh
While I work for scraps
So misinformed I see you swerving facts
Trying to keep it together like herding cats
Stuck in a bucket of thrashing hermit crabs
See one climbing up and try and herd it back
To watch it splash down in an unnerving crash

I don't see how working class
People with hurting backs
Can be so quick to run you down
Then turn around and circle back
Just to make certain your hurting bad

This won't work!
It's not the perfect path
What if I don't want to leave a tip
Like what If my foods cold
Or the service lacks?

So what if I act
Like an assertive ass
That makes the waitress pick
Between a tip and a nervous laugh
Walking out getting cold looks
From the rest of the service staff

While she still has to tip out
The busser, food runner, and bartender
Then go home and pay the gas bill
Otherwise it'll be a hard winter

Going through the ringer
Thinking if another mother fucker
Laughs and snaps his fingers
For me to bring him a coke
I'm coming in screaming to choke
Going for the throat
Or eyes to poke

Make another joke
About how I should be on the menu
I swear to god I'll end you
Like a geisha with a Ginsu
I'll pin you to the table
Next to your free breadsticks
Let you stand up dazed
Grab a chair for leverage
Then drop you with a head kick
Then grab your beverage and pour
It onto your crumbled body on the floor

Blood pumping adrenaline got me tipsy
Then walking out like who's coming with me

The manager tried to stop us
But he couldn't stop us all
Fuck storming Area 51

Let's rob the safe
Then hit the shopping mall
Head over to the bank
Breaking the locks installed
On the vault and dip out
Before the cops are called

At heart I'm a pacifist
I didn't want to fight
But I'll fight for fifteen
Living below the poverty line
Life is crippling but I'll fight
Despite the sickening
Feeling in my gut
Like a knife is sticking
Out of my abdomen
Referee called the foul's flagrant
Maintain I'm adamant
The price in blood
Is only a down payment

So if you add it in
Till you add it up
I'll send you back again
Till your backing up
Brinks trucks O' and add a bus
Packed with cash and cut
Diamonds and a bag of bud
I know your mad at us
Ask for good faith in negotiations
But we're lacking trust
After you ran us over

Then backed it up
Hit the gas and clutch
Burned rubber laughing
As we're hacking dust
Then ask if this half a cup
If full or empty
You got me about to
Get the mask and gloves
Grab a strap and slugs
I'm about to unload
Into his back, hat, and Ugg's
Watch as he's hacking blood
You sure that you've had enough?
Tired of 'em acting tough
But can't back it up
When we got the numbers
Like add 'em up
Not looking for an attaboy
Got you acting coy
We're ready to bash in heads
Or pay what you owe us back instead

#THEREVOLUTIONWILLNOTBETELEVISEDITWILLBETWEETED

I think the battle is lost
The world changes so fast
No matter the cost
Pay too much time
To the chatter and talk
Open wounds adding the salt
Accumulating baggage in bulk
Insults added bragging results
Quick reactions pre package your faults
I wish more people would just act like adults

Got to many people assigning blame
From racism politics or climate change
Childhood lessons my mind retained
Taught me we need to find a change
And not resign to maim but love instead

Acknowledge politics go above my head
It's all a crock of shit designed to
Divide and conquer the populace
From the profit rich pricks who insist
It's not greed for more stocks and topless chick
Or to pay for more helicopter trips to the opera
When half the world can't afford a pot to piss
But we'll spend a trillion dollars
On a fucking rocket ship
Because the planet is fucked
And they're trying to get off of it

Watch them throw a hundred mill at Noah's Ark
If there was a god he'd probably throw a spark
Of lighting down and watch it get blown apart
Then switch Ken Ham out for Jonah's part

People have never had access
To this much information
But most gets ignored
While they're spoon fed syndication
Reality now is imitation
I think we've been sentenced
To a penance of endless waiting
In a tenement of demented tenants
With a known history of contentious relations
The menace contend it's
Remnants of immigration
So I'm penning my penance
In these sentences wasting
My mother fucking breath

Cause y'all can't hear me though
Clearly those corporate cheering Joes
Coming from the top of the cage
Like a raging Rey Mysterio
Making more O's than Cheerios
Nearing those record profit margins
Give two fucks if you're shopping bargains
See the color red got you
Programmed to shop at Target
Your not the smartest
They BANK on that LITERALLY

This is now a sickly prophecy
In the form of a real life Idiocracy
Chased by a pimp named Upgrade
While the world acts obnoxiously

Possibly even one day
We'll overthrow the overlords
Hear the blowing horn
Sounding their retreat
While we're pleasantly
Lost in reveries
Like Luke reveling
Next to OB1 and Yoda's form
Hoping to find peace like Aegon
Returning to the frozen north
I hope we get there one day

#WOKE

Correct me if I'm wrong but
I think we have a penchant
When we're on Social Media
To get offended
The stream is endless
Going from two to ten cents
With our opinions entrenched
And thoroughly defended

Call me apprehensive
We act pretentious
Then expect this lack of tact
To snap defenses
Retaliate with an act of vengeance
Slinging insults like Shady
At the Rap Olympics

I'm guilty too of being a woke troll
Masked in comic relief
Some of y'all like

"You got nothing in common with me
I'ma just leave a comment to see
If he want this drama with me
You don't want no problem with me
I'm savage AF 💯"

This country is an open wound
Flesh gaping see the bone
Like an addict scratching
At a rash he can't leave alone
I hate to take such grievous tones
But once hatred's seed is sown
Someone needs to show some love

Maybe I should end this
Before I exceed a two minute read
Maybe if I up my friend list
I'll get a few more retweets

Like who uses poetry to speak to the masses?
Acting like he knowing me and my passion?
What kind of person use words instead of their actions
Aimed to heal instead of constantly clashing

Living like Clash of Clans
When World War Hat Trick
Happens apt to plan
Or Aliens happen to land
On what side of the battle lines
Do you happen to stand?

#SNOWFLAKE

You want to call me a snowflake
It's a bit cold hearted but ok
Juiced up like you've been sipping OJ
Going against my will like we're in probate
Try and cut me off then turn and pro rate
With your tirade doesn't matter if I'm gay
Straight or however I identify I'd say
It's none of your business get out my face

Turning to a crisis
I won't be a convert
Turn me to a convict
Over this conflict
Of course I'm concerned
These cons serve
A monster truck
Crushing civilization
Forgive my alliteration
It's a nervous tick
That gets worse
Closer to obliteration
Better bear arms
To your battle station
It's hard to tell
If this is an exaggeration
It's sad it's taken us
This long to mobilize
Broken hope disguised
As swollen pride
It's funny y'all hoping

Your soul survives
Yet live more spiteful
Than a poltergeist

If there is a god
His favorite thing is irony
You see my wrinkles
And try and iron me
You don't see how
These pitfalls create mountains
Where a pride of lions breed
Where we lift each other up like lion kings

You think I'm sensitive
Because I'm abhorred
By senseless shit
Like unjust sentences
Like 99 years for
Performing an abortion

The distortion of truth
For political gain
Opposition treated
Like a criminal gang
We seek freedom
You offer literal chains

Killing snowflakes using global warming
His cabinet filled with Goebbels swarming
Putting kids in concentration camps but

Seeking 👏 Asylum 👏 Isn't 👏 Illegal 👏

While the pauper prince is sitting regal
In a high chair throwing temper tantrums

This is embarrassing
On a global scale
We've gone off the rails
Get a mop 'n pale
Time to clean up this mess
We need to stop the sale
Of this country to these corporations
Who've got more skeletons in their closets
Than a fucking morgues basement

Fuck the banks, big oil, and big Pharma
Soon I hope you meet that bitch Karma
Money is their power it's time to disarm the
Powers at be give it to the people's army

#TROLLS

I'm guilty too
I'm a hypocrite
I'm not always above the fray
But I swear on Auntie May
If we keep upping the ante
The damage may be beyond reproach
We approach people's post
Like Lisa Lampinelli on a roast
My honest hopes is we stop
Mocking the opposition
How hard is it to stop and listen
Too busy going look at me!
Listen as I drop this wisdom
We got liberals mad at liberals
Cause they're not liberal enough
Christian's are mad at Christian
Cause they're not biblical enough
The differences in individuals
Is too minimal to be this cynical
We gotta change the narrative
This particular path is pitiful
I'd rather go like Pac then participate
Please allow me to articulate
The facts get lost in garbage and waste
With half the population on barbiturates
You reap what you sow
And the harvest is great
A harbingers garden of hate
People just stuck farther in place

Who cares?
They got no ducks in the race
They give no fucks to relate
Just looking for an excuse
To huff n puff in a rage
We gotta let go of our anger
Except Nazis... Fuck them
Trolls are cockroaches
The internet needs to fumigate
This useless fake human waste
Clueless nuisance using hate
In a lucid state thinking it's cute
Now they've scaled the walls
They're coming through the gates!
We need to change how we view debate
Calling each other stupid
As a crude escape
Turning rude with haste
Slinging death threats
In excess then turn
And act embarrassed
When they cue the tape
Of you spewing hate
Better go back start deleting tweets
Before you seek a priest to speak to
Like Jesus please my knees are weak
The ground is crumbling beneath my feet
I always heeded thee I believed the creed
Just don't judge my actions previously
I didn't really mean it please!
I'm sorry, that's your thing right?
Forgiveness?!?

#OLIVEBRANCH

I get it…
You thought he was a breath of fresh air
Now you're afraid to wear
A hat because the death stares
His message hit home
He even provided comic relief
Now some of ya'll got the bugle
Playing sounds of retreat
Layered over sounds of the grief
Of children ripped from parents
Degraded then locked in cages
Watch as he throws rocks in rages
Usually reserved for toddlers ages
Mock the sages drop the pretense
Lock up the pages
Of the Washington post
For saying that Washington's a joke

Look at the big picture
I'll tell you how we got here
Spinning out on the last turn
Like we're driving top gear
Watch him mock queers
Give his children top tier
Jobs at the White House
Lacking qualification
I'm asking you sympathize
With all the frustration
At the gall of this layman
Who calls for invasion

Of Iran to take the anger and angst and redirect it
He's gambling with soldiers lives to get re-elected
He's got a full tank and it's not hard to see it's septic
He's not for you he's for the rich just please accept it
He's one zany bat shit crazy megalomaniac
For fuck sake I'll even take Dick Chaney back

I gotta admit we gotta ditch
The golden snitch Moscow Mitch
He's getting rich like he's flipping bricks
Brings the Senate to a standstill
And could hardly give a shit
If first responders on 9/11
Are dying to fly in heaven
Because he wants to drag his feet

Politicians use the power of the people to leverage it
For their benefits then call social security a hand out
When every time I make or spend money
They got their fucking hands out

I don't mind paying taxes
If your fixing bridges and roads
Treat our tax money like a give and go so we can score
So we can feed the poor ease the sore feet of workers
On the factory floor the ones who need it more
Than congress asking for another fucking pay raise
It's gonna take more than a little tax break to placate
This next of round of elections we need you to vacate
The premises we'll find someone else to fix the blemishes

#DRAINTHESWAMP

I have a vote for sale
Do you want to buy it?
Don't play coy with me
You can't deny it
You dissuade the undecideds
Detest the other side with
Duress, derision, and mock any
Who don't fall in line with this side

So I'll let you pick which side that is
My vote is for sale!
Wanna try and pry it from me?
Soldiers are out there
Dying for me to be free
To elect the powers
That rule over me
Trying to get pull over me
So they can pull anything
Like rule overseas
To rule ovaries
Just need to do a meet in greet
In a back room with a cool notary

A hand shake later
Election security gets voted down
I'll let you buy my vote
But only if you vote to protect it

There's enough meddling
Since Citizens United

We got lobbyists denizens
Penning the laws
Writing their own regulations
Don't want the average citizen involved
Just install more apps to keep the tenements lulled
They do what they can to keep the innocents calm

Have I got it wrong?
You buy my vote and they pay for yours?
I'd like to renegotiate the rate for sure
I know I'm late of course
To negate the course
The country is a cruise ship
Moving with blatant force
To maintain a course
Towards imminent destruction
At the hands of immigrant hoards
Pouring over the border
As long as I get to watch
Another episode of hoarders
I'll accept the decay
Of the brick and mortar
This Country was founded on

The Statue of Liberty
Is a tourist trap of a forgotten age
The populace is lost in obnoxious rage
Mouths turned to pincers
Spitting toxic plagues
'Cause everyone is too right
To say they're wrong

I'll let you buy my vote
Pay for it not with words but with action
Promise me change then make it happen
Quit with the endless distractions
Raise the minimum wage to $15
Give the captains of industry a cap then
Quite showing us your teeth
Then giving me the ass end

My vote is for sale
I know it has value
I'll give you the price
I know it might wow you
My voice has power
I get 3 to 20 likes per post
I even got followers on either coast
I don't mean to boast

Let's just say
My opinion carries weight
And the country's scary place
So I want my voice to be heard.

Made in the USA
Coppell, TX
14 October 2024

38646836R00046